I0518291

October In New York

A Love Story

Lina Rehal

Lina Rehal

October In New York

A Love Story

October In New York © 2016 Lina Rehal

Published by Lina Rehal

Printed in the United States of America

ISBN: 978-0-9976150-0-5

Version 05.12.2016

Contact Lina Rehal

Email: rehalcute@aol.com

Website: www.thefuzzypinkmuse.com

Dedication

To my husband and best friend, Dick Rehal: Thank you for your support and encouragement, but mostly, for your love.

Special Thanks

To my beta readers, Kathie Moulison, Jo Capano and Christina Levine for the time and effort each of you put into reading the first draft of October In New York. Your comments and suggestions were a tremendous help.

To Mary Cooney-Glazer for the hours spent at Panera going over the many rewrites. Your input and editing skills through this entire journey have been greatly appreciated.

To my two writing groups, North Shore Scribes and Red Rock Rewriters, for listening to chapter after chapter and offering critiques and suggestions along the way.

To my budding fiction writer, my granddaughter, Katie Martin for pointing out a few things I missed. Teaching you about writing has taught me more.

"Love is hopeful.
It welcomes promises.
Like the changing seasons, it adapts."
Lina Rehal

Contents

Chapter One

Gwendolyn

Gwendolyn was surprised when Thomas called and asked her to meet him in Boston the following Friday.

"Harborfest is the last weekend in June. I want to do something special on your birthday. I booked a room for two nights at the Hyatt on the Harbor and dinner on Friday. We'll be able to see the fireworks from our table. Saturday, we can go to Faneuil Hall."

So like him. Makes plans and assumes I'm available. "It sounds wonderful and is sweet of you to remember my birthday, but I wish you had called sooner. I have plans for Friday."

"I know it's short notice. Is there any way you could cancel them? I have something important I want to talk to you about."

"What's wrong?"

"Nothing. We haven't seen each other in a while and I'd rather talk in person."

A while! I haven't seen him since the end of March, before he had his heart attack. Thomas didn't want her to visit him in Chicago. He promised they would spend time together soon, but his business and medical appointments always took precedence.

Until this phone call, she'd decided to end their futile, long distance affair. Gwendolyn was tired of living *her* life by *his* schedule. There was no future in it. Thomas would never leave his wife.

Gwendolyn only had to hear his voice to realize she couldn't break it off. She loved Thomas and wanted to be with him, no matter what.

"Can you at least give me a hint?" She asked.

"I miss you. Will you come?" It was all he needed to say.

"I'll be there."

Chapter Two

Gwendolyn

Gwendolyn wondered what was so important Thomas couldn't tell her over the phone. *Why does the man have to be so dramatic and mysterious? Maybe he wants to end it? He wouldn't do that on my birthday. Besides, he's made all sorts of elaborate plans. Thomas can be a little rigid, but he's a caring, gentle man and loves to surprise me.*

Gwendolyn hadn't dated much since her divorce. She wanted nothing to do with men, romantically – until Thomas.

She thought about the night they met. It was in October, almost four years ago. She went to New York City to do some shopping and visit her friend Sylvia, who owned a small gallery on the lower East Side. On the first night of her vacation, the two women had dinner together. They made plans for her to see Sylvia's fall exhibit in a couple of days. Gwendolyn returned to the hotel at nine-thirty. As she hurried toward an elevator, a tall man in a dark suit, already inside, pressed the button and held it open for her.

"Thank you," she said.

"You're welcome. What floor?"

Gwendolyn noticed his deep blue eyes and alluring smile as she stepped inside.

"Twenty-Two."

Leery of being alone in an elevator with a man late at night in New York City, she kept an eye on him and noted every detail in case she needed to identify him later. He was at least six feet tall, had a medium build, probably in his mid forties, clean-shaven and impeccably dressed. His wavy dark brown hair had touches of gray at the sides. *Oh, I'm being paranoid,* she thought. *He looks like a normal businessman and a handsome one at that.*

Just before they reached the seventeenth floor, a sudden jolt brought the elevator to a dead stop. Gwendolyn missed the handrail and fell against Thomas, almost knocking him down.

He steadied himself and helped her straighten up. She was hyperventilating. He seemed to understand her fear of enclosed spaces and injected a little humor in an attempt to help her relax.

"We must have hit a speed bump."

The alarm sounded as he pressed the button. "Oh my God, we're stuck," she said.

"I'm sure we'll be out in a few minutes. Grab the railing and take deep breaths."

Gwendolyn held the metal bar so tightly, her knuckles turned white. His gentle manner quelled her anxiety. She was thankful he was there.

"There's a phone in here. I'll see what I can find out."

Thomas spoke to someone who told him the elevator was stuck between floors.

"Yes, we know that," he said. "What are you doing about it?"

"The Fire Department and the elevator company are on their way. How many are in the car?"

"Just two."

"Are either of you injured?"

"No, but shaken."

After hanging up the phone, he held his hand out to her. "We haven't been properly introduced. I'm Thomas Winslow from Chicago."

His ability to remain calm in a serious situation impressed her. She wondered if he could see right through her with those sea blue eyes. "Gwendolyn North from Massachusetts."

"I go to Boston on business several times a year. Do you live near Boston?"

"Not too far from it. I live in East Gloucester."

"Isn't that where all the artists are?" He asked.

"Yes. I have a studio on Rocky Neck."

"What are you doing in New York?"

"I'm on vacation and visiting a friend who has a gallery here."

"A fun trip, then. How nice."

"Are you here on business, Mr. Winslow?"

"I own a software company in Chicago. I'm here for a convention. Please, call me Thomas. "

The hotel Manager called to let them know the elevator company was working on the problem and it could take a while. Thomas kept her occupied and even made her laugh. If he was worried, he never let it show.

"What if this thing falls before they can fix it?" Gwendolyn asked.

"Think positive thoughts."

"I'll try."

Taking a deep breath, Gwendolyn thought, *there positively has to be an easier way to meet nice men.*

An hour later, they heard the whir of the motor. Thomas helped her up from the corner of the floor where they had been sitting.

"Here we go," he told her. "Hang on tight."

Hotel staff, curious guests and two firemen were waiting for them when the doors opened. The Manager brought them to his office to fill out some papers. He apologized for the inconvenience caused by the incident and told both guests their bills were being taken care of. The crowd had dispersed by the time they returned to the lobby. It was a night she would never forget.

"I could use a drink," Thomas said. "I know it's late, but how about joining me in the bar? I'd love to hear about your studio."

Gwendolyn remembered wanting to learn more about him too. *Just my luck to finally meet someone who seems decent and he's from Chicago.*

"All right. Only for a little while."

Chapter Three

Thomas

Thomas was relieved when Gwen agreed to cancel her plans for Friday and meet him in Boston. He had a lot to talk to her about and needed to do it in person, not on the phone. *It was thoughtless of me and a bit selfish to call at the last minute and expect her to be available. I've taken too much for granted, but that's going to change.* His illness had kept them apart for too long, but Thomas was fine now and eager to be with the woman he loved.

Alone in his office, Thomas thought about Gwen. He missed the feel of her soft skin and the sound of her laughter. He remembered thinking how pretty she was that night in the elevator nearly four years ago and the frightened look in her eyes when she realized the danger they were in. He was sure part of her fear had to do with being alone with a strange man and had done his best to put her mind at ease.

Thomas was thankful they weren't hurt. Tired and wanting a drink, he decided to invite the pretty woman from the elevator to join him in the lounge.

After they filled out the incident forms, Thomas led Gwendolyn past the bar to a quiet booth at the back of the room. Several people turned and raised their glasses in the air as the couple passed by.

He folded his wrinkled jacket and placed it on the seat. "This is much better than the elevator floor. Are you comfortable?"

"Yes, but I must look awful. Will you excuse me while I visit the Ladies Room?"

"I think you look lovely. What would you like to drink? I'll order while you're gone."

"A glass of Merlot, please. I'll be right back."

A waiter rushed over. "Good evening. We're all happy you're both okay. Whatever you want is on the house."

Thomas was hungry and suspected Gwendolyn might be too. "Thank you. We'll each have a glass of Merlot to start. When the lady comes back we'll order something."

She returned a few minutes later. "Are you hungry? The waiter said whatever we want is on the house."

Laughing, she flipped her long, honey blonde hair behind her shoulders. "In that case, I'm starving."

It was good to see her relaxed. She was probably in her early forties, but could easily pass for thirty. Without the heels, he doubted she'd come up to his shoulders. Her jade green eyes were softened by the candlelight. Thomas knew he couldn't deny those eyes anything. He was intrigued and wanted to learn more about the attractive artist from the East Coast, even though nothing could come of it.

After a minimal amount of small talk, they moved on to more personal questions.

"Tell me about your studio. How long have you been there?"

"It's small but adequate. I've been there for eight years."

"You live there?"

13

"Yes. There's a three-room apartment on the second floor. Many of us live above our shops or studios."

"Do you live there alone?"

"Yes. Well, for the past three years, that is."

"Oh," he said. "What happened to your roommate?"

Gwendolyn hesitated before she answered. "He left."

He sensed it was a difficult subject for her. "I'm sorry. I didn't mean to pry."

"It's okay," she continued. "Eight years ago I married an artist, David North. We rented the studio and apartment for almost a year before we bought it. Three years ago, he ran off with one of his models."

"You didn't suspect anything?"

"I had my suspicions, but couldn't prove it. I never thought he'd up and leave like that. Shortly after our fifth anniversary, I came home one day and found his closet empty and a hand written note taped to my easel."

"G,

I'm sorry, but I couldn't go on pretending to be happy. You can have the studio. My lawyer will contact you about signing it over. David."

"No children?" Thomas asked.

"No. What about you? Any kids?"

"No."

She changed the subject. "Tell me more about your work."

"Not a lot to tell. I started the company twenty-two years ago, from the ground up. A one-man operation for the first few years, then it took off. Winslow Technologies has grown significantly. We now have one hundred and fifty employees, including salesmen and office staff. I travel a lot. It's been hard work. Still is. But, worth it."

"Sounds like you enjoy your work," she said. "The traveling must be fun."

"It's mostly for business and conventions, like this trip, or meeting new clients."

"It sounds great to me. I don't travel much. I like New York because of the art galleries, museums and shopping. I love the shopping. Have you ever been married?"

"Once." He offered no further explanation. "What about the theater? Any shows planned?"

"Once was enough for me too." She seemed to sense his uneasiness about the subject and moved on. "I'd like to see at least one play while I'm here."

Knowing she assumed he was divorced, Thomas let it go at that. "What else is on your itinerary this week?"

"There are a few things I'd like to see, of course, but I don't have any set schedule. I'll go back to my friend's gallery again and maybe visit one other. I want to shop on 5th Avenue. I kind of wing it."

"I envy people who can do that. I always have to have an agenda."

"Always?" She teased.

"Pretty much."

"My work has flexibility. You have a tight schedule in the corporate world."

15

"Yes," he said. "In my personal life as well. It's the only way I can manage both. I'm not good at spontaneity."

"I could never be that well-organized," she said.

Thomas laughed. "I like that about you. You're creative and spontaneous. I'm too regimented. Too much discipline can make a person seem dull."

"I don't find you dull at all. You're intelligent, easy to talk to and fun to be with."

"Thank you," he said. "I've enjoyed your company tonight too."

When they finished their second glass of wine, Gwendolyn glanced at her watch. "Look at the time. We've been talking for two hours. It's late. I should be getting back to my room and you must have to get up early."

"It's been an interesting night," he said. "I'll see you to your room. Don't want you in an elevator alone."

Thomas remembered escorting Gwendolyn back to her room that night. He knew it couldn't go anywhere, but saw no harm in inviting her to dinner. He wanted to see her again.

"I hope the rest of your week goes well. Thank you again for everything." She hesitated a bit. "Well, good night."

Thomas fought the urge to kiss her. He didn't want to scare her off. There was a slight awkward moment before he spoke. "I'd like to see you again. If you don't have other plans, would you have dinner with me tomorrow night? I know a great Italian restaurant."

"That sounds wonderful," she said. "I'd love to have dinner with you."

Chapter Four

Gwendolyn

After looking through her closet, Gwendolyn decided to buy a new dress to wear to her birthday celebration in Boston with Thomas. Trying to figure out what to wear, reminded her of the first time she went out to dinner with him in New York.

Thomas was already in the hotel lobby when Gwendolyn arrived at six o'clock for their dinner date. "You look lovely," he said.

"Thank you."

"The restaurant is only a couple of blocks from here. It's a nice night. I thought we'd walk, if you don't mind."

"I don't mind."

Thomas led her out of the hotel and onto the street. He asked about her day. She told him about shopping on 5th Avenue. He had a way of making her feel comfortable. She liked that about him.

When they arrived at the restaurant, she was surprised at how small it looked from the outside. They walked down three stone steps onto a tiny patio that had four tables set up for outdoor dining.

Once inside, the familiar aromas of garlic, basil and marinara sauce brought Gwendolyn back to her grandmother's kitchen. Thomas had chosen just the right place for their first date.

"It smells so wonderful in here," she said.

"You mentioned you liked Italian food. I figured I couldn't go wrong."

"Did I also mention I'm Italian?"

"No, you did not. But, I still think you'll love the food."

A tall man in a dark suit greeted Thomas. "Good evening Mr. Winslow. It's good to see you again."

"Good evening Antonio. Nice to see you too. This is my friend, Gwendolyn North."

"Welcome to Antonio's. Your table's ready."

They followed him to a rounded booth near the back of the room. Gwendolyn slid in next to Thomas. Antonio placed the menus on the table.

"Enjoy your dinner. Marco will be right with you."

"Thank you, Antonio."

She wondered how many other women he'd brought there.

He seemed to read her mind. "I come here a lot when I'm at a convention or seminar. Mostly business lunches."

"It's charming. I'm sure the food is great." *So what if he comes here with other women,* she thought? *He lives in Chicago and falls into the category of "geographically undesirable." I'll probably never see him again after this week.*

"They make the best ravioli. Do you like Chianti?"

"Yes, and I love ravioli."

"Welcome back, Mr. Winslow. Would you and the lady like to start with a glass of wine?"

"Thank you Marco. Yes. Please bring us a bottle of Chianti."

When the waiter walked away, Thomas turned toward her. "You're the prettiest woman I've ever met in an elevator."

"Oh, do you often meet women that way?"

"No. But, I did notice how attractive you are even before you stepped inside. When that car got stuck, I couldn't believe my good luck."

They both laughed. "Honestly, I don't know what I would have done if you hadn't been there last night," she said. "I was so scared. I'm glad you were there."

"I'll let you in on a little secret. You weren't the only one who was scared."

"Well, you fooled me. I thought you were wonderful. I was impressed by how you managed to remain calm in such a dangerous situation."

While soft violin music played in the background, they talked about chance meetings and fate. Thomas pointed out some of the scenic pictures of Italy that hung on the wall and told her which were his favorites.

When Marco returned, he opened the wine and poured some into a glass for Thomas.

"Excellent. Thank you. We'd like to wait a bit before ordering."

Marco filled their glasses and left.

Thomas smiled and raised his glass. "To chance meetings."

Gwendolyn couldn't deny the butterflies in her stomach every time she looked into those gorgeous blue eyes of his. She touched her glass to his and repeated his words.

When Marco returned, they ordered their meals. Thomas was right about the food.

"I haven't had ravioli this good in a long time. The sauce is delicious."

"I'm glad you like it," he said. "I'll make sure Marco tells the chef."

Gwendolyn enjoyed the meal and the wine, but mostly, she enjoyed the company. Thomas was confident, extremely attentive and well versed in almost any subject. He had an air of formality about him, which she thought was due to his upbringing. He seemed to get a kick out of her impulsive nature.

"I wish I could do things spur-of-the-moment," he said.

"I like surprises," said Gwendolyn. "I hate uniformity."

"Oh really?" He teased. "You didn't seem too crazy about the surprise that elevator gave you last night."

"You're right there. But, the outcome was a nice surprise."

"You got me on that one," he said.

"And you did something that wasn't on your agenda."

"But, it was. 'Nine-thirty p.m., meet pretty woman in elevator.' I always have a plan," he said.

"Do you always plan everything you do in such great detail?"

Thomas leaned forward. He stroked her face with one hand. "Not always. I've been known to act on impulse occasionally."

His lips were so close to hers, Gwendolyn could almost taste them. "Have you, now?" She said, in a low taunting voice.

There were no traces of formality in his kiss.

Chapter Five

Gwendolyn

Gwendolyn canceled the dinner plans with her friends for Friday so she could meet Thomas in Boston. Nick was disappointed, but Kate understood. She could always count on her friend to understand. Gwendolyn remembered telling Kate about the night she met Thomas.

Gwendolyn had returned to the hotel, after her date at Antonio's with Thomas. She checked her phone messages.

"Hi. It's Kate. Hope you're okay. Things here are fine. I fed Lucy and Ethel. Nick said to tell you he misses you. Call me."

Kate Ross was her best friend and the owner of Designs By Kate, the shop next door. Her unique creations were hand-made from beautiful glass beads and sea glass. Gwendolyn knew Kate would take good care of her goldfish, Lucy and Ethel, and look after the studio while she was away.

If a problem came up, Nick Marino, owner of The Ebb Tide Pub, could handle it. Nick worked on his father's fishing boat when he was younger. It didn't take him long to realize he wasn't cut out to be a fisherman. His dream had always been to open his own restaurant. He was a great cook, could fix anything and was always there when they needed him.

Between the drama in the elevator, shopping and her date with Thomas, Gwendolyn forgot about her promise to call Kate and let her know she'd arrived in New

York safely. Since it was after midnight, she decided to call Kate in the morning and apologize.

"I'm sorry I didn't call sooner. I had a bit of excitement my first night here. It was late by the time I got back to my room. I can't talk long. I'm going to Sylvia's gallery with Thomas."

"What excitement? Who's Thomas?"

"I got stuck in the hotel elevator for an hour my first night here."

"That's terrible. Were you hurt?"

"No, but, I was scared out of my wits."

"Why didn't you call me yesterday or last night? I've been worried about you."

"I went shopping on 5th Avenue and then out to dinner with Thomas. Time just got away from me."

"Who the hell is Thomas?"

"The man I met in the elevator."

"You went out to dinner with a guy you met in an elevator?"

"No, silly, the **gorgeous** guy I was stuck in the elevator with."

"He only knew you for an hour and he asked you to dinner?"

"Not exactly. It was more like three hours. We had drinks together in the hotel lounge after we got out of the elevator."

"Oh, well, that's different," said Kate. "You were practically old friends by then. So, who is he? What's he do? Where's he from? Where did you go for dinner? Don't tell me he's an artist."

"No, he's not an artist, but he knows a lot about art. He owns a software company in Chicago. We went to a lovely Italian restaurant. He's a great kisser and I really have to go."

"Wait. He's from Chicago? He kissed you? Wait till Nick hears this one."

"Yes, and yes. And, I know long distance romances don't work out. I really have to go. I'll call you in a couple of days. There's no need to tell Nick about any of this. He'll make way too much of it. Tell Lucy and Ethel I miss them."

"Okay. Keep me posted."

She loved Nick dearly, but as a friend. He liked playing big brother and was over protective of both women. She didn't need a lecture on the dangers of dating a stranger.

Gwendolyn had to hurry. She didn't want to keep Thomas waiting.

Chapter Six

Gwendolyn

Gwendolyn packed a pair of black pants, three tops and the new red dress she bought especially for her dinner in Boston with Thomas. He liked her in red. She tucked two pairs of shoes, a cosmetic bag full of toiletries and a few accessories into her suitcase. She had learned how to travel light and pack in a hurry.

Packing made her think about the many times she'd rearranged her own schedule to coincide with his. She thought of the weekends, long flights and last minute cancelations when something came up. Gwendolyn lived for the hours they spent together. She hated saying good-bye and having to leave him after each trip.

When they were together in March, Thomas talked about leaving his wife. Did she dare think that could be what was so important? He talked about it before, but always came up with a reason not to. He was afraid of what would happen to his company. He couldn't afford a divorce just then. Leah's father was ill. Her father passed away. It wasn't the right time. Gwendolyn started to think there was never going to be a right time. Then, Thomas had a heart attack.

When he wouldn't let her visit him in the hospital, Gwendolyn decided she'd had enough. She wanted a normal relationship. It was time she realized that was never going to happen and moved on with her life.

Carrying her suitcase out to the car, she thought about Thomas and their unconventional romance. She laughed at herself. *Who am I kidding? One phone call and*

I'm packed and on my way. The few years I've had with him have been the happiest of my life. I love him too much to give up on our relationship.

Gwendolyn started the car, turned on the radio, buckled her seatbelt and headed for Boston. She hoped his news was good.

Chapter Seven

Thomas

Thomas seldom acted on impulse, but secretly envied those who could. He followed a rigid work schedule and let too much of the businessman spill over into his personal life. All that got him was a loveless marriage and a heart attack.

He placed the last shirt into his suitcase, closed it, made sure he had his plane ticket and waited for the cab to take him to the airport.

At the terminal waiting to board the plane to Boston, Thomas tried to read the newspaper. Excited about seeing Gwen, he couldn't concentrate. They hadn't been together since late March. He had taken her back to Antonio's where they reminisced about their first date, laughing at how shocked she was when he kissed her right at the table.

He thought back to that first week in New York. The day after their dinner at Antonio's, Thomas skipped out on part of the convention and accompanied Gwen to her friend's gallery. He enjoyed discussing the exhibits with her. Later, they had hot dogs from a street vendor and went to a movie. He loved her spontaneity. It was a pleasant diversion from the structured life he lived. For the next few days, Thomas saw as much of her as possible.

On the flight to Boston, Thomas thought about his life, especially the events of the past few months. Before his heart attack, he had decided to leave Leah. Their twenty-five year marriage was a sham. The reasons for sticking with it no longer mattered to either of them. Before he could do anything about

27

it, once again, fate intervened.

One night after dinner, with the dishes still on the table, Leah told him she wanted a divorce.

"There's someone else," she said. "That shouldn't surprise you."

"No. I guess it shouldn't."

"Let's be honest. I know you have someone too. I overheard you talking on the phone a couple of times. I want to file the papers and move to Seattle as soon as possible."

She had caught him completely off guard. He couldn't believe what she was saying. His head was spinning. "There's a lot to consider. Have you thought about the financial part of this?"

"I don't want to ruin you financially, Thomas. This isn't about money. It's about finally being able to live our lives the way we want to. This marriage hasn't been easy for either of us. We deserve to be happy. I'll agree to turn my shares in Winslow Technologies over to you, if you agree not to go after any of my inheritance. We can sell the house and split the profit. I'm willing to negotiate on our other assets."

They came to an amicable agreement, had the papers drawn up and put the house on the market. He was planning to go to Boston and tell Gwen, when he had the heart attack.

She was terribly hurt when he wouldn't let her visit him in the hospital. Thomas hoped she would understand once he was finally able to explain his life to her and tell her his news.

The flight seemed longer than usual. Thomas took a short nap. When he woke up, they were starting their descent. It wouldn't be long before he'd see her again.

There were many more things Thomas wanted to know about the woman he loved. He knew she was beautiful, a talented artist, spontaneous and passionate. She loved Italian food, old movies and Renoir. But, he wanted to know the things two people in an ordinary relationship know about each other. Things like, when she bought a new dress, changed her hairstyle or sold a painting. He hoped it wasn't too late.

Thomas wanted to fall asleep every night with her beside him. He wanted her there when he woke up in the morning. He's wanted nothing more since the first time she fell asleep in his arms.

Chapter Eight

Gwendolyn

On the drive to Boston, Gwendolyn listened to soft rock. It brought back memories of the first time Thomas made love to her.

The day after their dinner at Antonio's, Thomas cut out of a lecture and went to Sylvia's gallery with her. He skipped as much of the conference as possible the rest of the week to be with her. He took her to Central Park, The Empire State Building and The Statue of Liberty. They had lunch at the Algonquin Hotel and ate dinner together every night.

On their last day in New York, they went back to Sylvia's gallery to say good-bye and stopped for an early supper. As a thank you, Gwendolyn insisted on it being her treat.

Thomas leaned across the table and covered her hand with his. "I've had a wonderful time this week."

"Me too. I loved seeing the city with you. Can you believe I've never been to the Statue of Liberty before? You're a great tour guide."

"I should be thanking you. I love art, but seldom visit a gallery when I'm here. Not much fun alone. I like Sylvia. She has some extraordinary exhibits on display. Mostly, I enjoyed your company."

Thomas hesitated before he went on. "I want to see you again. I do get to Boston on business occasionally. In fact, I might be seeing a new client there sometime in late November. If I let you know ahead of time, would you meet me in Boston? Or, maybe I could come to Gloucester? I'd love to see your studio."

"I'd like that."

"Great. Now, what would you like to do on your last night in the big city?"

Gwendolyn didn't care, as long as she was with Thomas. "Nothing fancy. Something low key."

"What about a walk? No particular destination. We can stroll along 5th Avenue and window shop or head toward Rockefeller Center? It's pretty at night. Stop for a drink along the way. Maybe catch a late movie?"

"That sounds wonderful. I'd love to go for a walk."

"You might want to go back to the hotel first and grab a sweater. It's warm now, but it could get cooler when the sun goes down."

"Good idea. They said it might rain later tonight."

"If it does, we'll take a taxi back."

She paid the check and they went back to the hotel.

Gwendolyn slid the keycard into the slot. When the green light came on, Thomas opened the door to her room and followed her inside.

"Nice. Pretty good size for a hotel room in New York City."

"They made a mistake. My room wasn't ready at check-in. I had to wait, so they upgraded me to a superior king with a view of Times Square. The mini-fridge has come in handy.

"Not bad."

31

Gwendolyn dropped her purse on the sofa and walked toward the bathroom. "I just need a minute to fix my makeup. Make yourself comfortable."

"Take your time."

When she returned, he was standing in front of the floor-to-ceiling wall of windows looking out. She watched him for a minute. He looked more relaxed than he had all week. Maybe it was the royal blue sweater and tan chinos. She liked this casual side of him.

Her heart beat a little faster at the sudden realization they were alone in her hotel room. *What am I worried about? He's been a perfect gentleman all week. A bit too perfect. Damn! Why am I thinking these things about a man I might never see again after tonight?*

He turned and faced her. "I love watching the people down there. All going in different directions. All in a hurry."

Gwendolyn grabbed a light jacket from the closet and hung it on the back of a chair. She walked over and stood next to him.

"New York is such an exciting city. I'd love to come more often, but I can't afford to travel much."

That gave Thomas an idea. "Would you really like to come here more?"

"Oh, yes. I'd like to visit other places too. Maybe even Paris someday."

He placed his hands on her shoulders and looked at her. "I don't want this to end. I think there's something special between us. I want to see you again. If I could arrange a weekend and send you a ticket, would you meet me here?"

She hesitated, but not for long. "I'd like to see you again too, but I don't feel right about letting you pay my way."

"Why not? We enjoy each other's company. "We love going to dinner, the theater and galleries. We'll always wonder what might have been."

She didn't want it to end either. When Thomas pulled her closer and kissed her, Gwendolyn knew she wanted more.

He had another idea. "How about staying a couple more days?"

"Are you serious?"

"Two more days. What do you say? I'll cancel my meeting."

"Okay. Let's do it."

"Wonderful! We can go back to Central Park and take that horse and carriage ride we didn't have time for."

Gwendolyn was excited about spending two more days with him. "Maybe we can see another play?"

The hotel was happy to accommodate them. They changed their flights. Thomas canceled his business meeting and made a dinner reservation at Antonio's for the next night.

Once they were done making calls, he brought her over to the window again. "Storm clouds. It's kind of late for a walk now and it looks like rain."

"We could go to the lounge for a drink. Maybe it will just be a quick shower and by then we'll have thought of something else to do."

Thomas already had something in mind. "We could stay right here."

Was he suggesting what she thought? "Here in the hotel, or here in my room?"

He slid his arms around her waist, pulled her up against him and kissed her. His need for her was apparent. There was no mistaking his intentions. Reaching up, she wrapped her arms around his neck and gave in to her own needs.

Still holding her, he said, "I can think of lots of things to do on a rainy night."

"I have the feeling you are about to do something spontaneous."

"Not really. I've been thinking about it since I kissed you that first time in Antonio's."

"You mean you planned on coming back to my room and seducing me tonight?"

"No. You needed your jacket."

"So, I invited you to my room and the opportunity presented itself?"

He kissed her neck. "You could say that. But, the truth is, I've been thinking about making love to you all week. Imagining what it would be like."

She had been having the same thoughts. "Maybe it was a little premeditated on both our parts."

"Sounds like we've both been doing a lot of thinking. "

They stood holding each other for several minutes before he let go of her. "Why don't I call Room Service and order us a bottle of wine?"

"That would be lovely."

Gwendolyn hung her jacket back in the closet while Thomas ordered a bottle of their best Pinot Grigio. She was glad he thought of it. A glass of wine would help her relax.

While they waited, Thomas fiddled with the radio.

"Let me see what I can find for music. Oh, here we go, soft rock."

After Room Service delivered the wine, Thomas hung the Do Not Disturb sign on the outside of the door and dimmed the lights. He opened the bottle, poured two glasses and handed one to Gwendolyn.

"Let's have it over by the windows," he said.

"All right."

As the ominous clouds rolled in, they raised their glasses and shut out the noise from traffic and the crowded city below.

"To two more days and whatever else fate has in store for us."

After the tiny clink of the glasses, they sipped their wine. He wrapped one arm around her waist and kissed her cheek. She leaned in closer to him and looked out at the darkening sky.

"Looks like a thunderstorm's brewing," said Thomas.

"Lightning scares me and it can be a bad omen."

"You're superstitious?"

"About some things."

35

She detected a hint of superstition in his voice too. "We should take advantage of the calm before the storm. Let's move away from the window."

He led her to the sofa and set his glass on the table. "I'll close the curtains."

Thomas sat down next to her and poured more wine. "Feel better?"

"Much, thank you."

When she finished her second drink, Thomas took her glass and placed it next to his. He moved closer to her. Resting one elbow on the back of the sofa, he leaned forward and started stroking her arm with his other hand. His touch ignited feelings in her that had been dormant for a long time. As he gently kissed her neck, the protective wall she had built around herself began to crumble.

She needed to clarify things. "It's been a long time since I've been with someone. Not since my husband. I wouldn't want you to think I do this all the time."

"If I thought that, I wouldn't be here. It's been a while for me too. This isn't something I typically do on a business trip."

"I don't think that. You're too nice a person."

The wine lessened her anxiety. She blocked out the low rumbles of thunder in the distance and heard only his voice. "I want you, Gwen."

Thomas held her close, rubbing his arms up and down her back. She was attracted to his good looks and gentle manner. He brought out a passion in her she didn't know existed. His kindness and patience led her to believe he would be an unselfish lover. She threw her arms around his shoulders, dug her fingers into the soft fabric of his sweater and forgot about omens.

When he let go of her and stood up, the storm was right over them. But, she didn't feel afraid when she was with him.

"Are you okay?" He asked.

"Yes. I'm glad we're not out there."

He turned off the lights and reached for her hand. "Come with me."

He led her across the room. Standing by the bed, he kissed her again. She could taste the wine and caught the woodsy scent of his cologne.

"I have strong feelings for you, Gwen. I knew it the first time I kissed you. It's more than a physical attraction. I feel like a different person when I'm with you. I meant what I said about not wanting it to end. It won't be easy, living so far apart, but I think it's worth a try."

"I think so too."

He kissed her again and began unbuttoning her blouse. She shivered slightly when he slid it down her arms and tossed it onto a chair.

"Are you cold?"

"No, but you must be hot in that sweater."

Thomas pulled his sweater off, threw it on the chair and pulled her close to him. He ran his hands over her smooth skin and kissed her bare shoulders. "You're so soft and beautiful."

She liked the sensation of his bare chest against her and the feel of his strong arms. Gwendolyn needed him as much as she could tell he needed her.

Lina Rehal

Thomas turned down the covers. He lifted Gwendolyn onto the bed. Standing over her, he slowly finished undressing her and then himself, before getting into bed.

Loud claps of thunder boomed and lightning flashed through the curtain. Their passion was stronger than the tempest going on outside. Gwendolyn was not prepared for the storm that was yet to come.

Chapter Nine

Thomas

After spending the night with Gwendolyn, Thomas went back to his own room to shower and change. Later, he met her in the hotel restaurant for breakfast.

The waitress hurried over with fresh coffee. "Thank you. We need coffee," said Gwendolyn.

The girl gave them a few minutes to look at their menus. When she returned, they ordered bacon and eggs.

Thomas didn't talk much during the meal. Intermittent pangs of guilt riddled his thoughts.

"You're quiet this morning," she said. "Didn't you sleep well?"

Not ready yet to tell her what was eating away at him, he lied. "I'm just tired. I was thinking about some business calls I have to make before we go off for the day."

"I feel a bit guilty taking you away from your work."

"You're not the one who should feel guilty."

"What?"

"Oh…nothing. I just meant you didn't do anything wrong. I'm the one who forgot about a client. But, I'll call him and smooth it over."

"Have you thought about what we might do today?" She asked. "The weather has cleared up nicely. It looks like a beautiful day."

Distracted by his torn feelings, he hadn't heard a word she'd said. "I'm sorry. What did you say?"

"Are you all right? You seem preoccupied. Are you having second thoughts about last night?"

"No, of course not. Last night was wonderful."

"What then?" She asked. "I know something's wrong."

"Don't let it worry you. Finish your breakfast."

"Maybe you should go make those calls and meet me later?"

He had to tell her what was bothering him. *She deserves to know the truth about me. But, how can I explain my deceitful behavior? I can't tell her everything. How can I make her understand?*

"I'm sorry. You're right, but I need to go back to your room first. I left some papers I need on the desk."

"That's fine. I have some calls to make myself."

When they got back to her room, Gwendolyn looked on the desk. "Are you sure you left them here? I hope the maid didn't throw them out."

"Gwen, I need to talk to you. There aren't any papers. I said that so we could be alone. There's something I have to tell you."

"What is it?"

"Can we sit down?"

Her face paled as she walked toward the sofa. "This sounds serious."

"It is. I haven't been totally honest with you."

"What do you mean? What haven't you been honest about?"

Now he was the one whose heart was racing. He sat next to her and spilled out his confession.

"First, I want you to know that I care a lot about you. This past week has been the best one of my life."

"I care a great deal about you too. Please tell me what it is."

There was no easy way to tell her. He blurted it out. "I'm married."

It took several seconds for her to digest what she had just heard. "Married! You're married? And it didn't occur to you to mention that fact before now?"

"I'm sorry I didn't tell you sooner."

"You're sorry. I thought you were divorced. You knew that and you let me think it. You've been lying to me this whole time. You let me care about you. I trusted you and you think being sorry is enough to make it right?"

"No. I know it isn't, but I don't know what else to say. In the beginning, there was no need to tell you. Then I was afraid to."

Gwendolyn stood up. "Damn straight you were afraid! You were afraid I wouldn't go to bed with you!"

With a sudden strike, she caught his cheek and part of his jaw with her open hand. She hit him so hard his head snapped to one side.

"How could you do this to me? How could you spend a whole week with me? I wish I had never set foot in that elevator!"

41

Gwendolyn moved to the other side of the coffee table and kept her back to him.

Dumbfounded, he rubbed the side of his face. "I never meant to hurt you."

Turning toward him, she lashed out again. "Just what did you mean when you made love to me?"

"I meant everything I said to you. I do care about you."

"You wanted to fly me to New York when it was convenient for you, have your fun and then go back to your nice life in Chicago? You call that caring about someone? What about your wife? And, don't tell me she doesn't understand you! I don't understand you. I don't understand how you could do such a thing. I want nothing to do with you."

"My wife and I live separate lives. It's been that way for a long time."

"Don't give me that," she continued shouting. "It's your excuse to sleep around."

"No! It's not like that. I'm not like that. It's complicated."

She lowered her voice. "No, it's not. It's not complicated at all. It's simple. You're a liar and a cheat."

Thomas was tired and angry with himself for what he had done. *What was I thinking getting involved like that? I had no right. I should never have let it go that far.* He began to raise his voice as well. "I can't get into the details of my circumstances, nor would I expect you to understand the way I live. But, you have to believe my feelings for you are genuine. Last night meant a lot to me.

I'm in love with you. I knew it that day on the bridge in Central Park."

"Love!" She began shouting again. "How can you say that? What do you know about love?" Pointing to the door, she screamed, "I never want to see you again! Get out!"

"Gwen, please listen to me. If I wasn't in love with you, why would I tell you the truth now?"

"Just go."

Chapter Ten

Gwendolyn

Reminiscing about the night Thomas first made love to her also brought back the memory of the terrible argument they had when he told her the truth about himself. Gwendolyn remembered the way things ended and the anger she felt toward him. Standing with her back to Thomas after ordering him to leave her room, she heard him say, "Good-bye, Gwen," just before the sound of the door closing behind him.

She flopped down on the chair, covered her face with her hands and let the tears flow.

When she was all cried out, Gwendolyn tried to pull herself together. She went into the bathroom, washed her face and held a cold, wet cloth over her swollen eyes for a few minutes. Her ghastly reflection in the mirror brought her anger back to the surface. *What was I thinking, getting involved with a man I met less than a week ago in an elevator? How could I believe words of love from a stranger? Am I really naïve enough to believe he meant things said in the heat of passion? Maybe I'm just plain stupid. I believed David loved me and look how that turned out.*

She pulled her cell phone out of her purse. There were several messages from Thomas. *What part of 'I want nothing to do with you?' doesn't he get?* She had no intention of returning his calls. Instead, she called Kate.

"Hey, Gwen, how are you? I thought you'd be home by now. Don't worry. When I didn't hear from you I went over and fed your   fish."

"My plans changed, but they've changed again. I'll be home on the next flight out of here I can get."

Kate could tell her friend was upset. "What's wrong?"

"Nothing. I planned on staying a couple of extra days, but changed my mind."

"This wouldn't have anything to do with Elevator Guy, would it? When I talked to you two days ago, you were having a wonderful time."

"Oh, Kate." Gwendolyn burst into tears. "We had a terrible argument. Kate, I hit him."

"You've never struck anyone in your life. What did he do to make you that angry? Did he hurt you?"

"He lied to me! I trusted him and all the time he was lying to me."

"You hit a man over a lie? Take a deep breath then tell me what he lied to you about."

Gwen wiped her eyes with the back of her hand and took a deep breath. "He's married. I thought he was divorced. Yesterday he talked me into staying in New York two more days. We changed our flights and hotel accommodations. This morning he told me he's married. We had an awful fight. I told him I don't ever want to see him again."

"All right, so the guy lied about his marital status. That's not a first. You had a few dates with a married man. You didn't know he was married. It's not your fault he's a liar. At least you found out in time. It's not like you slept with him or anything. Oh…my…God! You slept with him."

There was a long pause. Gwendolyn didn't answer.

"It's okay. I understand. You must care about the scumbag if you let it go that far. Listen to me, honey, you book the first flight home and call me back with the flight number and time. I'll pick you up at Logan."

"Thank you. You're the best. I'll call you with the information, but I can take a cab from the airport."

She booked a five o'clock flight to Boston and packed the rest of her things. Afraid she'd bump into Thomas, she ordered a late lunch and ate in her room before checking out.

Gwendolyn walked toward the line of yellow taxis parked at the curb. Handing her suitcase over to the doorman, she gave him a tip and got in the car. He told the driver to take her to the airport, thanked her and closed the door. Just as the cab was about to pull away, she looked out the window and spotted him on the sidewalk waiting for the next taxi. "Good-bye Thomas," she whispered.

Chapter Eleven

Thomas

As he sat in the terminal waiting to board the plane for his flight back to Chicago, Thomas thought of Gwen and the argument they had that morning after he revealed the truth about himself.

Thomas had returned to his room after Gwen told him to leave. Still feeling the sting from her slap, he looked in the mirror. He had never been hit by a woman before and found it hard to believe one that small had so much strength. In the mirror, he saw the redness on his cheek and looking into his own eyes, saw the hurt in hers. He knew the redness would go away, but the look of betrayal would stay with him.

Gwen wouldn't answer his calls and didn't return the messages he left on her cell phone. Not that he blamed her. In hopes she would call and agree to see him, he booked a late afternoon flight back to Chicago and hung around the hotel until it was time to leave.

As Thomas waited in line for the next available taxi, he spotted Gwen getting into a yellow cab up ahead. He wanted to call out and try to stop her, but knew he had to let her go.

Once on board and in the air, Thomas settled in. When the flight attendant came around, he ordered a glass of wine, hoping it would help. It didn't. He saw Gwen's face in the clouds from his window seat and raised the plastic glass to his lips. *To chance meetings. Good-bye Gwen.*

47

After a second drink, Thomas fell asleep. He dreamed of Gwendolyn. "I trusted you!" She shouted at him, over and over. "How can you say you love me?"

Thomas woke up in a cold sweat. *Damn lies! Damn Leah! Damn me for not being man enough to get out of the farce of a marriage I'm in!* He got up to stretch his legs, went to the bathroom and washed his face with a cool wet paper towel.

He tried to read, but images of Gwen kept popping into his head. He remembered the frightened look in her eyes when she realized they were trapped in the elevator and how focusing on her anxiety helped alleviate his own.

Thomas was just about to take out his laptop and check his emails when the captain made an announcement.

"Ladies and gentlemen, we'll be experiencing some turbulence for the next half hour or more due to rough weather up ahead. We ask that you remain in your seats with seatbelts on. Please stow all laptops and bags in the overhead bins or under your seats until further notice. Thank you."

Thomas locked his tray table in the upright position and fastened his seat belt. *The last thing I need is more turbulence in my life,* he thought.

He heard a voice beside him. "Storm clouds," said the young woman next to him.

"What?" Thomas asked.

"I hate thunderstorms. I'm afraid of lightning."

"Don't worry," he told her. "I've flown through a lot of them."

Gwen was afraid of lightning too. She said it could be a bad omen. Thomas didn't believe in omens, but he

48

believed in fate. If the elevator hadn't malfunctioned, she would have gotten off on her floor and he wouldn't have given it another thought. He knew in his heart they were meant to be together and it was his own stupidity that destroyed what they might have had.

He leaned back into the seat and watched the beads of rain slide down the window. As the plane bumped up and down through the darkening sky, Thomas thought about how happy he had been less than twenty-four hours ago. *Maybe Gwen was right about lightning.*

Chapter Twelve

Thomas

When he returned home from New York, Thomas couldn't concentrate on his work. Images of Gwen filled his head. He tried to let it go, but couldn't stop thinking about her. He scrolled through the pictures on his phone and smiled at one of her on the carousel at Central Park. They both laughed as they rode the colorful horses like a couple of kids.

"This is a side of you I haven't seen," she said.

"You bring it out in me. You make me want to live in the moment."

He paused at one taken on the Gapstow Bridge. The beauty of the fall foliage and the view of the skyline from that spot excited her. She reached up and kissed his cheek. "It's just like in the charcoal in Sylvia's gallery. Thank you so much for bringing me here!"

He wrapped his arms around her and kissed her in the middle of the bridge. At that moment, Thomas knew he was falling in love.

Looking at the picture, Thomas knew he had to try to fix things between them. She wasn't answering his calls. There had to be something he could do. Something meaningful she would really like. An email would be too impersonal. Flowers were too easy. If he wrote a letter, she might not read it. He scrolled to the photo again. *That's it! The bridge. I'll send her the sketch of the Gapstow Bridge. She might not accept a package from me. I'll need to contact Sylvia to make sure she still has the drawing.*

Thomas explained some of the situation to Sylvia. It took a bit of coaxing on his part, but she finally agreed to help him. "I can't thank you enough," Thomas said. "I'll overnight you a check and enclose a note to Gwen. You tape it to the back of the frame and send the drawing to her, making it look like it's from you."

"She's a good friend. I'm happy to help. I hope you know what you're doing. I don't want to see her hurt."

"Neither do I."

"Good luck. Stop by the gallery when you are in New York again."

"I will."

Thomas hoped he was doing the right thing. He wanted Gwen in his life, even if they could be nothing more than friends. He had to at least try.

Chapter Thirteen

Gwendolyn

Two weeks after Gwendolyn returned home from New York, she received a Special Delivery package from her friend Sylvia. She tore off the brown paper and found the charcoal sketch of a scene from Central Park.

"The Gapstow Bridge," she said aloud. The one she admired the day Thomas went with her to the gallery. She wondered why Sylvia would send it to her. She didn't know its significance.

As she ran her fingers over the simple black frame, Gwendolyn felt something behind it. She turned it over and found a sealed envelope with her name on it taped to the back. She recognized the handwriting. It wasn't from Sylvia.

"Dear Gwen,

Words can't express how sorry I am. There is no excuse for what I did. I never meant to deceive you. The hours I spent with you were the happiest ones I've had in a long, long time.

I wish I could explain all the circumstances of my lifestyle, but I can't. I don't blame you for feeling the way you do about me now. I hope, in time, you can forgive me.

I asked Sylvia to send the drawing, as I thought you might not accept a package from me. I remembered how much you liked it. I hope you will hang it in your studio and think of our day in Central Park. Whether you believe me or not,

I knew I was falling in love when I kissed you that day on the bridge.

I will be in Boston on business just after Thanksgiving. I'd love to take you to lunch. I'll call you next week. If you don't want to see me, I will understand.

All my love, Thomas"

Gwendolyn read the letter three times. *Why is he doing this? Why doesn't he just leave me alone? Is he trying to alleviate his guilt or is it possible he is in love with me? Why do I care?*

She tucked the letter under the corner of the blotter on her desk and picked up the sketch. Her heart ached, as she remembered the first time she saw it.

During their dinner at Antonio's, Gwendolyn learned Thomas had a genuine interest in art. She thought it would be fun to have someone to discuss the exhibits with and invited him to go to Sylvia's with her the next day. He left the conference early and met her in the lobby of the hotel.

Sylvia greeted them when they arrived. She hugged Gwendolyn. "It's good to see you. I'm so happy you're here."

"Me too."

"And, you must be Gwendolyn's friend from Chicago," she said extending her hand to Thomas. "I'm Sylvia Turner. Welcome to my gallery."

"Thomas Winslow. It's a pleasure to meet you Ms. Turner."

"Please, call me Sylvia. I'm glad you decided to accompany Gwendolyn today. I hope you'll stop in to see us again."

"I'm sure I will."

Sylvia gave her friend another quick hug and headed back to her office leaving Gwendolyn to show Thomas the gallery. They discussed their thoughts on each piece as they made their way around. Like her, his taste in art was on the simpler side.

Halfway through the tour, she asked, "What do you think so far."

"It's smaller than others I've been to, but your friend has made good use of the space and natural lighting. She has some excellent pieces on display. I'm impressed."

"Sylvia takes great care in choosing each piece. She's had several good reviews on her exhibits and on the gallery in general."

"I can see why. Do you do watercolors?" He asked.

"Sometimes. Mostly I work in oils. I love working on a canvas."

"I'd love to see your work. Maybe the next time I'm in Boston, I can make a side trip to Gloucester."

Not sure how she felt about that, Gwendolyn didn't comment.

"Oh, look at that one," she said, pointing to a small charcoal hanging inside an alcove. If he caught her avoidance of his suggestion, he didn't let on.

"Central Park," he said. "The Gapstow Bridge. It's a beautiful spot."

"Looks like a pretty place," Gwendolyn commented. "I love it. It's simple and understated, yet it grabs your attention. It makes me want to be there."

A half hour later, they left the gallery energized and hungry.

"Come with me," Thomas said, taking her by the hand. "You haven't eaten in this town until you've had a hot dog from a sidewalk vendor."

Laughing, she followed him to the nearest stand. "I love hot dogs."

They found a bench not far from the vendor's spot and sat down to eat.

"This is the best hot dog I've ever eaten," Gwendolyn said, as she took another bite.

Thomas couldn't stop talking about the gallery. "It's more fun when you can share the experience with someone who appreciates art."

"I agree. I'm so glad you enjoyed it."

"What piece was your favorite?" He asked.

"The charcoal of the bridge in Central Park."

"Have you been to Central Park?"

"Once, several years ago. But, I don't remember seeing that bridge."

"I'd love to show it to you. How about tomorrow? I'll give you a personal guided tour. Bring your camera. That bridge has the best view of the New York skyline. You can get some great photos and paint your own pictures. I'll show you Bow Bridge, Belvedere Castle and Strawberry Fields."

"It sounds wonderful, but don't you need to be at a conference?"

"Just the morning lecture, but it's early. I can cut out on the rest and be ready to leave by ten. We'll have lunch at Tavern on the Green and ride the carousel if it's open and if there's time, we can take a horse and carriage ride. What do you say? Meet me in the Lobby of the hotel at 10 a.m.?"

"How can I turn down such a charming tour guide? It's a date."

Thomas was already in the Lobby when she got there.

"Good morning. Are you ready for the grand tour?"

"I've been looking forward to it," she said.

They took a taxi to 59th Street. "We can walk from here," he said.

It was a perfect fall day. She wondered if he was able to control the weather and ordered it especially for them. Taking her by the hand, Thomas led Gwendolyn to the bridge. The rich colors of autumn made her senses come alive. She noticed the vibrant reds and brilliant shades of orange fluttering in the breeze. With the slightest wind, they danced on the ground before her, spinning in little whirlpools with each soft gust. She snapped picture after picture, not wanting to miss one speck of this picturesque place.

The view from the bridge was spectacular. The tall buildings with the magnificent beauty of nature in the foreground made for some amazing photos. She took pictures of Thomas with the skyline in the background.

"I knew you'd love it," he said.

"It's absolutely breathtaking. Thank you so much for bringing me here!" On impulse, she stood on her toes and kissed him on the cheek.

"You are more than welcome," he said. "But, the tour has only just begun." Taking her hand again, he pulled Gwendolyn close to him, slipped his arms around her waist and kissed her."

Her senses were alive all right and it didn't all have to do with falling leaves and pretty colors. Standing on the bridge with Thomas holding her and leaves swirling at their feet made Gwendolyn wish she could set up her easel right there, capture the rich colors of autumn surrounding the stone structure on canvas and keep the memory of that day forever.

As she hung the drawing over her desk, Gwendolyn tried to tell herself he might not call, but wondered how she would react if he did. A relationship with him, like the carousel they rode in the park, had nowhere to go. Why did she let memories of him infiltrate her thoughts?

She missed him.

Chapter Fourteen

Thomas

Thomas thought about Gwen every day since he returned home from New York. He was so pensive, even Leah noticed.

"Is something wrong?" She asked, one night at dinner. "You haven't been yourself since you got home."

"I have a lot on my mind. A lot of work to catch up on."

Leah wondered what happened on his trip. Her husband was always preoccupied with work, but this was different. He looked sad and worried. She suspected it had to do with a woman, but didn't ask.

Thomas hoped sending Gwen the sketch of the bridge hadn't been a mistake. He was sure she had feelings for him too and thought the drawing of the bridge would soften her. He wanted so badly to see her again.

He kept thinking about their last day together and their last night, the night of the storm. It made her happy when he suggested they stay two more days. He played it over and over in his mind: The change in the weather. Her agreeing to stay in the room. How the lightning scared her. The way she reacted when he touched her. The feel of her lips. How he liked holding her and making her feel safe. The sound of thunder and flashes of lightning while they made love. The sweet scent of Freesia on her pillow. She wanted *him* as much as *he* wanted her. He was sure of it.

Thomas knew he should have told Gwen the truth about himself right from the beginning. Now, he had to pay for deceiving her. Overwhelming feelings of guilt came over him every time he remembered the argument and the betrayed look in her eyes. He wondered if she'd ever be able to forgive him and hoped she would agree to meet him for lunch.

He gave her a week to think about it before he called.

Chapter Fifteen

Gwendolyn

Since reading Thomas's letter, Gwendolyn could think of nothing else. She wondered what she would say to him when he called. She was about to break for lunch when her cell phone rang.

Recognizing his number, Gwendolyn picked it up and sat down at her desk. "Hello."

"Hi. It's Thomas. How are you?"

The familiar butterflies danced in her stomach at the sound of his voice.

"I'm fine. How are you?"

"I'm okay. I've had a busy work schedule."

"Busy is good." *What a stupid thing to say*, she thought.

"I wanted to call and apologize again, but I wasn't sure you'd talk to me. Not that I would have blamed you. I remembered how much you liked the charcoal of Central Park. I hope you weren't angry I asked Sylvia to send it. I was afraid you wouldn't open it if it came from me."

"I was a little at first. But, thank you. It was my favorite piece."

There was a slight pause before he spoke. "I remember every minute we spent together. I know there's no chance of a relationship between us, but I hope we can at least be friends. I really would like to see your paintings sometime and I'd love to take you to lunch when I'm in Boston. No strings, just friends."

"I don't know. I really don't think that's a good idea."

"I understand," he said. "Didn't think it would hurt to ask. So, did you hang the picture?"

"Yes," she said, "I hung it over my desk."

"I'm glad to hear that." He hesitated. "If you change your mind about next week…"

She didn't want him to hang up. Was it really wrong to have lunch with a friend? He does have an appreciation of art. He'd love Rocky Neck. She was rationalizing. The truth was she wanted to see him again.

"Thomas…wait."

"What is it?"

"Maybe there's no harm in lunch. Would you like to come here? There are several great restaurants and I think you'd enjoy the studios… if you have time."

"I'll make time. I'd love to visit the studios, especially yours. I'll add a day to my trip and call you later with the details. Is there any day that is not good for you?"

"Any one will work for me, as long as I know a few days in advance."

"That's great. I'll get back to you by tonight. And Gwen, thank you."

She hoped she hadn't made a big mistake.

Chapter Sixteen

Gwendolyn

Gwendolyn stepped back from her easel to view her work. Pleased with her current masterpiece, she began to clean her brushes. At the sound of the door opening, she turned and saw Kate walk in, holding a plate of cookies.

"Hi," said Kate.

"Good afternoon. How's business?"

"Practically non-existent, which is why I have time to bake. What work-in-progress are you into now?" Kate asked.

"None. I finished it. Are those chocolate chip?"

Kate put the plate down and moved closer so she could see the painting. "So that's the Gapstow Bridge in Central Park? The one where he says he fell in love with you?"

"That's the one."

"It's fantastic. The colors are so vibrant and alive. It looks like a beautiful place to fall in love. The couple kissing on the bridge really put it over the top."

"It is a romantic spot," said Gwendolyn with a sigh. "I had mixed emotions about the couple, but people add life to a painting."

"I'll say," said Kate. "So, have you accepted his invitation for lunch?"

"Yes. He's coming here the Wednesday after Thanksgiving."

"He's coming here?" Asked Kate. "That's great. I can't wait to meet Elevator Guy."

Gwendolyn laughed. "Stop calling him that."

"That's a week from tomorrow. Where are you going to go for lunch?"

"Probably Nick's. He has the best clam plates and lobster rolls."

"Good choice. Nick is dying to meet him too."

Gwendolyn made a fresh pot of coffee to go with the cookies and took out a pad of paper and a pen. The two women went over last minute details of the Thanksgiving dinner they were going to have with Nick and a few of the other shop and restaurant owners.

The closer it got to Wednesday, the more she stressed over his visit. *It's just a lunch,* she repeated over and over to herself. *Nothing more.*

Thomas called her from Boston on Monday. "I'll be with a couple of clients today and most of tomorrow. I can be in Rocky Neck by ten on Wednesday, if that's a good time for you."

"That's perfect."

Now, to get this place looking festive by Wednesday.

Nick helped her drag two trees and boxes of ornaments out of her storage closet. He set the four-foot tree up in her living room and the tabletop one in a corner of the studio.

"You're on your own as far as decorating. I'm not good with that stuff. Where's the picture you wanted hung?"

"That's okay. Kate and I can handle the lights and ornaments. She'll be over later. The painting is upstairs. I want to hang it in the living room."

"I'm getting my exercise today," he said.

Nick was in his early forties, six feet tall, had jet-black hair and dark brown eyes. Next to Kate, he was her closest friend. Because of his good looks and flirtatious nature, Nick was popular with the ladies around town. They all liked him, but knew better than to get involved with him romantically. Margo Peterson had a short romance with him that ended when she found out he was seeing a woman in Rockport. Gwendolyn and Kate liked his wild tales of adventure about the life he led before Rocky Neck, not to mention some of the more recent ones.

Nick followed her back up to her apartment. When he saw the painting of the bridge, he gave Gwendolyn a nod of approval. "Nice job, Sweetheart. This guy doesn't deserve you. You belong with a steady, dependable, good-looking, single fellow who appreciates your talent."

"And, just where do I find this perfect man?"

"You're lookin' at him," Nick said, turning toward her. "It's no secret you're special to me."

Gwendolyn gave him a friendly hug. "You're special to me too. But, we both know it wouldn't work. You could never be a one woman man."

With one arm still around her, Nick brushed her hair away from her eyes. "For the right woman I could."

"If only that were true, Nick."

Knowing she was probably right, his tone changed back to that of her protector. "Well, he'll have to answer to me, if he makes one more wrong move with you."

64

Chapter Seventeen

Gwendolyn

At exactly ten o'clock, Gwendolyn heard a car door slam. She glanced in the mirror and smoothed her hair one more time. The bell that hung over the door jingled, as Thomas entered the studio. Mesmerized by his sea blue eyes, she waited for him to speak.

"Hello, Gwen. It's wonderful to see you again."

"Hello. It's good to see you too. I take it you had no trouble finding the place."

That was intelligent, she thought. *Of course he had no trouble. He arrived right on time.*

"No trouble at all." Putting his gloves in his pockets, he scanned the room. "Your studio is charming. I see you're all ready for the holidays. Do I get the grand tour?"

"Oh, I'm sorry. Let me take your coat and then I'll show you around. You can almost stand in one spot and see the whole place."

She hung his coat on the rack and started with the front area. "I display my most current work in this front section."

"That seascape is absolutely beautiful," he said. "Where is it?"

"That's Good Harbor Beach. I did it at the end of the summer."

Next, Gwendolyn brought him to the back of the room where she had some framed older pieces hanging on the walls. Smaller, unframed canvases were stored in bins and stacked in corners. On her easel was a half painted lighthouse. "That's a commission I'm working on."

"And, who have we here?" He asked, seeing the fish tank. "You didn't tell me you had any pets. Goldfish, right?"

"Yes. Lucy is the red fish and Ethel is the golden yellow one. I usually don't talk about them much. People seem to be more interested in dogs or cats."

"I have an aquarium in my office. Tropical fish. Watching them is a great way to relieve stress."

"You didn't mention your pets either," she said.

Thomas followed her back to the front of the studio, stopping short when they got to her desk. "You did hang it."

"Yes."

"We were so happy that day on the bridge," he said.

She stopped him before he went any further. "I made coffee. Why don't we have a cup and then I'll show you the shops. My friend Kate wants to meet you. She owns the one next door. I thought we'd have lunch at the Ebb Tide. The owner is a good friend of mine."

"Sounds like you're the one with an agenda today. I'd love coffee."

She didn't include her apartment in the tour and was grateful he didn't ask. They had coffee and muffins in the studio and talked about his two days in Boston. She caught him looking at the sketch a couple of times and could only imagine the thoughts it evoked. It brought that day back to her whenever she looked at it.

"I like your studio. It's professional, yet it has warmth and a rustic charm. Your work is incredible. You're an extremely talented artist."

She wondered what he'd think of the painting she kept upstairs, deliberately out of sight. Part of her wanted to show it to him, but she couldn't bring him up there.

"Thank you," she said. "More coffee?"

Memories of him kissing her on the bridge flashed through her mind. Gwendolyn wondered how she would react if he tried to kiss her now.

"No. I'm all set," he answered.

Thomas offered to help with the dishes. Standing that close to him would have made her uncomfortable. "You sit and relax. I'll only be a few minutes. We'll stop by Kate's first or I'll never hear the end of it."

"Whatever you say. You're the guide today."

When she finished the dishes, they headed next door.

Kate greeted them with a big smile. "Good morning. Come on in."

"Thomas, this is my good friend, Kate Ross. Kate, this is Thomas Winslow."

"It's a pleasure to meet you," he said. "Gwen has told me all about you and your beautiful jewelry." Seeing her fiery red hair, he understood how Gwen's goldfish got their names.

"It's nice to meet you too. Can I get you anything? Coffee?"

"No thank you," he said. "We had coffee at Gwen's. I would like to look at your jewelry though."

Thomas looked at Kate's designs and commented on several pieces. He pointed to a pair of earrings in the case. "Those are lovely. Would they be an appropriate gift for a sixteen year old girl?"

Kate took them out of the case so he could get a closer look. "Yes. These are blue lace agate. The sky blue color is said to promote peacefulness and clear the mind. Do you have a daughter?"

"No, a niece. My brother's girl. She's my Godchild. These match her eyes. Here, I'll show you."

Thomas took out his wallet and showed the two women a picture of a pretty blue-eyed teenager.

"She has your eyes," said Kate.

Thomas laughed. "That's what my brother always says."

Kate wrapped the earrings and thanked him.

"We have to go," said Gwendolyn. "I have some galleries to show him and then we'll be at Nick's for lunch."

"Again, it was nice to meet you," he said.

"Same here and I hope you'll be back to see us soon. Say hi to Nick for me."

For the next hour and a half, Gwendolyn led Thomas in and out of the different shops and studios and introduced him to her friends. It was one o'clock before they knew it.

"Are you hungry?" He asked. "Want to stop for lunch now?"

"Yes. It's later than I realized. Nick's is right across the street."

They walked into the Ebb Tide Pub and were seated at a table with a view of the water.

"This is great," said Thomas.

"The food's even better."

Nick came out of his office and walked over to their table. "Hey, Gwen. I see Bobby gave you a good table." Before she had a chance to say anything, he reached out his hand to Thomas.

"Nick Marino. You must be Gwen's friend from New York. I've heard a lot about you."

"Thomas Winslow. I'm from Chicago. Gwen and I met in New York."

"Oh, yeah. She told us about the elevator incident. That was a close call. Good thing you were there."

"Yes, it was," said Thomas. "I'm glad I was there too."

Nick caught the look of warning from Gwendolyn. "Well, enjoy your meal. Maybe we'll see you again sometime." He turned toward Gwendolyn. "Let me know if you need anything, Sweetheart."

"I'm sure everything will be fine." Gwendolyn was annoyed with Nick and glad when he went back to his office. She hoped Thomas didn't pick up on his hostility.

The rest of their lunch was perfect. Nick stayed out of the way. They ate and appreciated the view, limiting their conversation to the weather, food, art and other safe subjects.

"You were right," Thomas said. "These clams are great. The chowder is one of the best I've ever had."

After lunch, they went for a walk before heading back to her studio.

"Your friend Nick is an interesting character. Did I detect a bit of jealousy?"

"I'm sorry he was so rude. That's not like him. It's not that he's jealous. He has no right to be. We're good friends, nothing more. Nick thinks it's his job to protect me. He does it to Kate too. There's no excuse for his rudeness. I will be talking to him about that."

"I guess he was just looking out for you. It's obvious he cares for you a lot."

Thomas turned and faced her. "I've had a great time today. Being with you again has been wonderful. You know I'd like it to be the way it was in New York, but if it can only be friendship, I'll accept that. I won't pressure you for more."

Gwendolyn didn't know what to say. She wanted what they had on the bridge too, but she kept remembering the last time they saw each other. "I'd like that too, but I don't think it's a good idea." He took her hand in his. She didn't pull it away. They turned and walked back to her place without another word.

Thomas took his coat off and hung it on the rack. He rubbed his hands together. "It's a bit chilly in here."

Gwendolyn locked the door and made sure the "closed" sign was in the window. "I'll turn up the heat. I have an electric fireplace upstairs. I'm going to get another one for down here this winter. They really help in small areas like this. Would you like coffee or something to drink?" She asked. "A diet soda or water? I have a bottle of Merlot in the back room. If you have time, that is."

"My flight isn't until early tomorrow morning. I'm in no hurry. I'd love a glass of wine, if you'll join me."

"Make yourself comfortable. I'll be right back."

She returned with the wine, two glasses and a corkscrew. "Let's have it at the table. I'll let you open it."

Thomas poured the wine and handed her a glass. "To friends."

Gwendolyn doubted either of them would be able to keep their relationship on that level, but she repeated his words. "To friends."

"I've been admiring your work. You're one talented lady. You must get a lot of commissions."

"Thank you. I do get a good number of them. Sylvia wants to include my work in her spring exhibit."

"That's fantastic! I will definitely go see it. I'll be able to tell people I know the artist."

"Sylvia would love to have you visit."

Thomas glanced toward the wall over her desk. "Do you mind if I ask you a question?"

She knew what he was going to ask. "What is it?"

"That day in Central Park. All the photos you took. Did you paint any of them?"

Gwendolyn couldn't hide it any longer. She had to show him Couple On The Bridge.

She grabbed the bottle and her glass. "Come with me."

When they got to the top of the stairs, she flipped on a light and led him to the middle of the room. Gwendolyn put the bottle down and brought him closer to the sofa.

"I finished it last week. What do you think?

His expression told her what she needed to know.

"The Gapstow Bridge," he said. "It's the most beautiful work of art I've ever seen…and, the most meaningful. Why didn't you show it to me earlier?"

"I was afraid."

"Of what?"

"Of what you'd think. How it would make you feel."

Thomas turned toward her. "I knew I was falling in love with you that day. I don't need to look at a painting to remind me." He put his arms around her and kissed her. "I think you feel the same way. You said it on canvas and you say it with your eyes."

"You're right," she said. "I'm in love with you and I don't believe we can spend time with each other as friends."

"No. We both want more than that."

She cut him off. "But, it can't be more. You're a married man."

"I know. I swear, what I told you about my marriage is the truth. And, I know it's a lot asking you to trust me, but we'll work things out. Just give us a chance."

Gwendolyn needed to believe him. Not able to deny her feelings any longer, she refilled their glasses and took Thomas by the hand. "Would you like to see the rest of the apartment?"

Chapter Eighteen

Gwendolyn

Gwendolyn led Thomas to her bedroom that chilly day in early December, knowing there would be no turning back. When he made love to her, she knew no right or wrong, only that she loved him and wanted to be with him. Nothing else mattered.

Later, she made sandwiches and coffee. They could see the Couple On The Bridge from where they sat in the kitchen.

"The painting is beautiful. You did a great job on it. How come you didn't hang it in your studio?"

"Thank you," she said. "I didn't want to share it. I like having it in my living room. It gives me a warm feeling."

"Speaking of warm, you were right about the electric fireplace," he said. "It really throws a lot of heat."

"I want to get a smaller one for downstairs. It helps with the heating bills."

"I guess I'd better be going," he said. "I'd stay, but it wouldn't look good to your neighbors. Don't want to give them something to talk about."

"That's for sure. It's a small community. Hard to keep secrets around here."

"Before I go, I have something to ask you."

"What is it?"

"I have a business meeting in New York in a couple of weeks. It's on a Friday afternoon. If I send you a plane ticket, would you join me for the weekend? I thought you could go shopping or visit Sylvia and meet me later. We could go to dinner at Antonio's Friday night and walk around Rockefeller Plaza on Saturday. The city is lovely at Christmastime."

She answered without hesitation. "I'd love to see New York at Christmastime with you."

Chapter Nineteen

Gwendolyn

A few days after Thomas's visit to Rocky Neck, Gwendolyn received a round trip ticket to New York City. He booked a room at the hotel where they met. She looked forward to spending the weekend with him.

As promised, Thomas took her back to Antonio's. Antonio remembered her. He seated them at the rounded booth near the back again. On their way back to the hotel, it started to snow.

"Now it'll look like Christmas," he said. "I hope you brought boots."

"I did. I tend to over pack. Never know what I might need."

Saturday morning, they took a cab to Central Park. The brilliance of fall had been replaced with a thin blanket of snow.

"This is wonderful," said Gwendolyn. "Now I can paint a snow scene of the bridge."

Thomas was right. Christmas in New York was beautiful. She loved the displays in the store windows on 5th Avenue.

"They're so pretty and festive."

"Wait till you see it at night."

After a light lunch, Thomas suggested they head back to the hotel to rest before dinner.

"I have reservations at a steak house I think you'll like," he said. "Then I thought we'd walk around Rockefeller Plaza, look at the lights and maybe catch the ice skaters. We can stop for a drink somewhere later."

"That sounds great. You really would make an excellent tour guide," she said, laughing.

The rest of the night was perfect. They had a romantic dinner, watched the skaters and enjoyed the holiday atmosphere. On the walk back, they stopped for a nightcap. Thomas had one more thing on his agenda.

Gwendolyn went to the Ladies room. When she returned, there was a small box wrapped in teal blue with a white bow on it next to her drink.

"What's this?" She asked.

"It's for you," he answered. "Merry Christmas, Gwen."

"You didn't have to get me a present."

"I wanted to," he said. "Go ahead. Open it."

When she opened the blue Tiffany box, the diamond cuts in the gold bangle bracelet glittered in the dim lighting. She could hardly speak. "It's...it's beautiful."

"I hope it fits," he said. "Try it on."

She slipped it over her hand and onto her wrist. "It's so sparkly. Look at how it dances in the light."

She leaned forward and kissed him. "Thank you. I love it. But, you really shouldn't have."

The gold bracelet was the first of several expensive gifts.

Gwendolyn's return trip to the Big Apple marked the official beginning of their unconventional romance. She knew the odds of this relationship lasting were not in her favor.

They were opposites. Thomas was formal, confident and reserved. Gwendolyn was free-spirited, casual and spontaneous. She knew he could be a bit controlling, but he was the kindest, most generous man Gwendolyn had ever known. She loved him and believed, as he did, that things would work out.

Chapter Twenty

Boston

Thomas sat in the lobby of the Hyatt, anxiously awaiting Gwendolyn's arrival. When he spotted Gwendolyn coming through the big glass doors, he rushed over to greet her.

"Gwen!" He hugged her and stepped back to look at her. "You look wonderful. It's so good to see you. Happy birthday."

His excitement overwhelmed Gwendolyn. She needed to get her bearings. He barely gave her a chance to speak.

"Thank you. It's good to see you, too. You're looking well. I can't believe we're finally together."

"It's been too long," he said. "But, all that's going to change. I've already checked us in. We can catch up later."

As she looked around, Gwendolyn wondered what he meant by his comment. "This is lovely," she said. "Have you been waiting long?"

"No. I only got here an hour ago. I put my luggage in the room, grabbed a newspaper and decided to wait here. You must be tired after the drive. Let me take your bag and we'll go upstairs."

"I would like to freshen up and change before dinner."

"We have plenty of time. Follow me."

Gwendolyn was impressed with the room. The king sized bed looked comfortable and inviting. She loved the earth tone colors of the décor.

"This is a nice room. There's even a mini-fridge."

She saw the long-stemmed red roses in a clear glass vase on the table. "Those can't be from the hotel."

"No. The roses are from me. Wait till you see the view." Thomas walked over to the large window and drew the long white curtains open. "Here's the best part."

"Oh, how beautiful," she said. "What a fantastic view of Boston Harbor!"

"It's a great city," he said. "I love Boston."

Gwendolyn dropped her purse on the bed and threw her arms around Thomas. "I've missed you. Thank you for all this and for the roses. I've been so worried about you. Are you tired from your flight? Do you want to rest before dinner?"

"I'm fine. I napped on the plane. The only thing I want before dinner is you."

He kissed her the way he'd been wanting to since he saw her in the lobby. They were almost late for dinner.

79

Chapter Twenty-One

The Birthday Dinner

Gwendolyn had never been to this restaurant. She loved the mahogany woodwork and the elegant look of the tables draped in white linen beneath cobalt blue plates and sparkling silverware. Delicate flowers and dimly lit oil lamps added to the ambiance. They were seated at a table by the wall of windows, facing the harbor. A bottle of imported champagne was chilling in a gold bucket.

"This is wonderful," she said.

"I knew you'd like it."

Thomas always seemed to know instinctively what she liked. He knew her so well.

Once settled, the waiter opened the champagne and filled their glasses. "I'll be back to take your order when you're ready."

Thomas raised his glass. Instead of one of his usual toasts about health, wealth or happiness, he touched his glass to hers with a clink and said, "To us."

They never drank to "us" before. That was new. He picked up on her hesitation.

"Is something wrong?"

"No. To us."

As always, Thomas had chosen an excellent champagne. The light, tiny bubbles tickled her nose. They sipped in silence for a few minutes, each thinking of the other.

Gwendolyn leaned forward in her chair and rested one arm on the table. She gazed out the window at the spectacular view. Boats moved about the busy waterfront below in anticipation of the fireworks scheduled at dusk. Police vessels whizzed by. Their blue lights flashed across the rippling water, as the gorgeous colors of sunset spread over the Atlantic.

Her thoughts shifted to Thomas. She had the feeling there was something different about him. He lost at least fifteen pounds since she last saw him and had a few more streaks of gray, but that wasn't it. It wasn't something physical. He seemed more relaxed. Maybe that was it.

Thomas marveled at her youthfulness. At forty-five, Gwen could pass for mid-thirties. Her hair was a bit shorter now and curlier. She was wearing a long, red sleeveless dress and the gold bangle bracelet he gave her. He loved her in red and wondered if she bought it for tonight.

"You look lovely. Is that a new dress?"

"Thank you. Yes," she answered, happy that he noticed.

"I want tonight to be special. Happy birthday, Gwen."

The alcohol calmed her nerves, but it did nothing for her impatience. "Thank you. It's sweet of you to do all this for my birthday. I really do appreciate it. But you said you have something important to talk about. We haven't seen each other in close to three months. You asked me to change my plans because you have something to discuss. When are you going to tell me what this is all about?"

"I'm sorry. I don't mean to be mysterious. Not anymore. It is important. It's important to me and I hope to you too. I promise I'll explain everything after dinner."

81

Before she could ask more questions, the waiter returned. They ordered filet mignon and Caesar salads. He refilled their glasses, retrieved the menus and sped off to the kitchen. Thomas would tell her when he was ready. Gwendolyn went back to her champagne and private thoughts. Sometimes his rigidity annoyed her.

Thomas was eager to tell her his news and anxious to see her reaction, but didn't want to tell her during dinner. "It's good to be together again. I've missed you. Let's enjoy our dinner. Then we'll talk."

She never could resist his smile. He went out of his way to make her birthday special and it was wonderful to finally be with him. She decided to relax, enjoy the meal and his company. "I've missed you too. I'm happy you can travel now. How are you feeling?"

"I feel terrific. I've been walking three or four times a week. Lost eighteen pounds."

"I noticed. You look great."

They kept the conversation light, making it a point to stay on safe topics.

"How's your filet?" He asked.

"Delicious," she answered.

"How's Kate?"

"Fine. She said to say hello."

The meal and service were both excellent. Everything, so far, was perfect.

Thomas had waited so long for this. He planned the evening down to the last detail, saving the best part for the fireworks.

Chapter Twenty-Two

Gwendolyn and Thomas

The big orange glow began to disappear into the horizon.
People gathered below. Some spread blankets on the lawn,
while others positioned chairs on the pavement. More boats
scurried about in search of the perfect spot to view the
fireworks display that would soon explode over the harbor.

Gwendolyn was ready to explode too. "We've
talked about the restaurant, the meal, the view and the
weather in Chicago. I've told you about the painting I'm
working on and you've told me about new software. Please
tell me what this is all about. Are you tired of our
relationship?"

Shocked by her assumption and a bit annoyed,
Thomas wasn't sure how to respond. "Is that what you
think I wanted to talk to you about? You think I arranged
all this and flew to Boston to end it between us. I can't
believe you'd think I would do that to you and on your
birthday."

"I'm sorry. I don't know what I'm thinking
anymore. I know you wouldn't do such a thing. You went
through a lot of trouble to make this a special night and
here I am getting angry. Please, just tell me what it is. I
can't stand the suspense."

All the scenarios about this moment he had
rehearsed in his mind escaped him. Thomas looked at her
and quietly stated, "Leah has left me."

It took her a few minutes to grasp what he had just
said. When she recovered, Gwendolyn didn't know what to

say. For almost four years, she hoped Thomas would leave his wife. She never imagined it would be the other way around. He talked about leaving Leah after her father died, but so far, it had been just talk. He hadn't acted on it. He was worried that a divorce would ruin him financially.

"I can't believe it. What happened?"

"She left me for someone else."

"Leah left you for another man?"

"No," he hesitated. "A woman. She left me for her aerobics instructor." He looked down at the dessert menu, not really seeing it.

Gwendolyn was stunned. "Did you have any idea of this?"

"Yes. A few years after we were married, I could tell things weren't right. She couldn't hide it from me anymore so she finally told me the truth. We were both afraid of what might happen if anyone ever found out. It was different back then. She was a teacher at a prestigious school for girls and afraid of losing her job. Her father would have disinherited her if he knew the truth. He was a rich and powerful attorney. She got him to back my business. I was worried about what he'd do if I left her. And, there was my pride and my ego. We agreed to stay married but live separate lives. That's the way it's been between us for many years."

"Why didn't you tell me about Leah a long time ago?"

"I wanted to, but I couldn't. After her father died and she got her inheritance, I decided to leave her. She beat me to it. I wanted to tell you then, but I saw no reason to drag you into it. I planned on coming to see you as soon as I could to tell you all this."

"What happens now? Will you get a divorce?"

"We are divorced, Gwen. It became final last week."

"What? Why didn't you tell me sooner? I can't believe this! How could you keep that from me?"

Surprised by her anger, he tried to tell her the rest. "A lot was going on. We filed for the divorce and started getting the house ready to put on the market. I had a lot of legal matters to tend to."

"And a phone call would have been too much? What, didn't it fit into your plan?"

The waiter appeared again and asked what they would like for dessert.

"I don't want dessert, but I could use a drink," she said.

Knowing what she liked after dinner, he ordered. "We'll have two Sambuccas, straight up, please," he told the waiter. "And two cups of black coffee."

Thomas gave her a few minutes to compose herself. He couldn't blame her for being upset. He wished he hadn't picked a public place to tell her this, but he thought she'd be happy about it. He thought she'd understand his reasons for not telling her when it all happened.

When the drinks came, he went on with his revelation.

"I wanted to tell you then, but not over the phone. I needed to put the past and my life in Chicago behind me first. My only plan was to sell the house, give Leah her half and move on. I was going to come to you and tell you everything. What didn't fit into my plan was the heart attack."

85

She interrupted him. "That's another thing! If it was all over between you and Leah, why couldn't I have come there?"

Thomas continued. "I was with Leah when I had the heart attack. We were cleaning out the garage. I was filling boxes with items we planned to donate and ignoring what I thought was heartburn. She noticed I was sweating and rubbing my chest and told me to sit down. I never made it to the chair. I collapsed just as she was calling 9-1-1. If Leah hadn't recognized the symptoms and acted quickly, I might not be here."

Gwendolyn shuddered at the thought of how close she had come to losing him. "Thank God she was there and knew what to do."

"Leah postponed her move and helped me get through it. We didn't love each other, but we didn't hate each other either. When I got home from the hospital, we had a long talk. She realized living like that must have been as difficult for me as it had been for her and thanked me for not exposing her all those years ago."

"As soon as I was on the road to recovery, Leah left for Seattle. She had her inheritance from her father and agreed not to go after any part of my company. We sold the house and split our other assets."

Gwendolyn poured a little more Sambucca into her coffee and took a sip. Her anger had subsided. She didn't want to cause him any more stress. He had been through enough. "What about now?"

"I'm working on opening an office in Boston. I think it will prove to be a great location for many reasons. It will be a smaller branch and less work for me. Less traveling. My Chief Operating Officer is going to handle

Chicago. I started laying the groundwork months ago. I didn't want to mention it until I had more definite details."

"You have had a lot going on. I meant what about your *health* now?"

"My doctor says I'm doing fine. It was a wake up call, though. I'm going to be fifty on my next birthday. I know what I want out of life. I've known for almost four years. I've procrastinated far too long. I don't intend to waste another precious minute."

"I'm sorry I was so impatient with you," she said. "I understand now why you needed to talk in person. I'm glad you didn't tell me all this over the phone."

"Maybe I shouldn't have told you here in the restaurant," he said. "I wanted this to be a special night for both of us."

"It has been," she said. "Just being with you has made it a very happy birthday. Now, I want to see those fireworks you promised me."

"There's still a few minutes before they start," he said.

She had the feeling there was something else he wanted to say.

Chapter Twenty-Three

Gwendolyn

The harbor was dark now. The first few rounds of fireworks lit up the darkened sky with vibrant colors of red, white and blue. Bursting into the air, they cast their reflections on the buildings below. Higher and higher they went, their magnificence cascading over the harbor. They shimmered like gold dust as they dissipated in a downward plunge toward the sea.

Thomas took her hand. Gwendolyn was right. He had one more thing to say to her. "Tell me it's not too late for us."

Not sure of exactly what he meant, Gwendolyn hesitated before she spoke. Was he about to offer her the relationship she waited so long for, or was he going to suggest another convenient arrangement?

"What are you asking me?"

He reached in his pocket, took out a tiny blue velvet box and placed it in front of her. "I want to spend the rest of my life with you."

She knew why he had come to Boston.

Thomas waited until she opened the box before he continued.

Gwendolyn gasped. The pear shaped diamond, in its platinum setting, sparkled more than the show going on outside.

"It's so beautiful. Thomas, it's gorgeous."

He smiled at her reaction. "Then you like it?"

"I love it! And I love YOU!

"It hasn't been an easy relationship. I've made a lot of mistakes. I promise I will never lie to you again. I love you, Gwen. I'm asking you to marry me."

Did she dare believe this wasn't a dream? "I've wanted this for so long, but never thought it would happen."

Thomas took the ring out of the box and placed it on her finger.

"Will you marry me?"

Somewhere between the thundering booms over Boston Harbor and the synchronized explosions of brilliant colors in the sky, Gwendolyn said, "Yes."

About The Author

Lina Rehal, a self-published author known for her short stories and nostalgic pieces, has always wanted to write fiction. Since her retirement in early 2015, she has found a new "voice" in writing romance stories by combining her passion for fiction and love of storytelling.

October In New York is her first novella. It is available on Amazon.com in both print and Kindle versions. She is currently working on her next book, Loving Daniel.

Ms. Rehal is the founder and facilitator of North Shore Scribes, a writing group for women. Her first book, Carousel Kisses, a collection of personal essays and poems about growing up in the late 1950's to early 1960's, is available on Amazon.com in both print and ebook versions.

Contact Lina Rehal

Email: rehalcute@aol.com

Website and Blog

www.thefuzzypinkmuse.com

www.carouselkisses.blogspot.com